Margaret Stuart Barry lives in Richmond in Yorkshire, and had a wonderful time writing about the Attic Toys, who are all based on her favourite friends from childhood! Of course more toys are always pushing into her memory, wanting to be included – so watch out for more stories!

Tessa Richardson-Jones drew the pictures, and now has all the toys living on her desk!

The attic toys

MOGGY

THE WITCH'S CAT

MARGARET STUART BARRY

Pictures by Tessa Richardson-Jones

for

Patrick Heagerty

First published in Great Britain in 1995.

Bloomsbury Publishing PLC, 2 Soho Square, London W1V 6HB.
A CIP catalogue record for this book is available from The British Library
ISBN 0 7475 2231 6 pb
ISBN 0 7475 2264 2 hb
Text design by AB3.
Printed and bound in Great Britain
by William Clowes (Beccles) Ltd,
Beccles and London.

• CONTENTS •

• CHAPTER ONE •

Moggy, The Witch's Cat

MOGGY WAS the attic cat. Of all the toys, he was the meanest. His black fur was not shining, as it should have been, but was dusty and lumpy. He had one whisker on either side of his nose and couldn't remember what had happened to the others. They had probably been snapped off in some fight or other.

"Well, I don't care what anyone says," said Prissy, "I quite like him." He wouldn't win a prize in a Cat of the Year show, but he's one of us."

Prissy was the doll who was too-good-to-be-true, and lived in the grandest house in the attic – except for Mayor Bungle's, of course. Not far away, lived her friend, Tilly Losh the rag doll.

Prissy and Tilly met in the café for morning coffee and a bit of a chat. Tilly

was a careless, cheeky sort of a doll, but she had all the best gossip, and that is what Prissy loved. She pretended, of course, not to be interested in what other people did. But she was.

"Have you noticed," Tilly Losh was saying, in between mouthfuls of buttered teacake, "that Moggy is getting very prowly lately?" Prissy hadn't.

"Do you think he's up to something bad?" she asked, hopefully.

"He might be," said Tilly. "I think we'd better watch him."

Watching Moggy was something interesting to do. They followed him around at a distance. The two dolls noticed that he didn't buy his food from Mrs Bizzy's shop, the way everyone else did. He scrummaged around in everybody's bin instead.

"What a cheek!" gasped Prissy, as Moggy scooped out half a cream cake from hers.

"You didn't waste all that food, did you?" cried Tilly Losh. Then she blushed red as the cat found a cucumber sandwich with only one bite out of it in her own bin. "Goodness knows what the greedy animal will find in the mayor's bin!" she said.

Moggy went home and fetched a large shopping basket and leapt into Mayor Bungle's bin. He was there quite some time. When he came out he had two whole

chickens, half-a-dozen roast potatoes, a pawful of stuffing, half-a-dish of strawberry jelly, a bottle of fizzy drink and a slice of toast and marmalade.

"Isn't that absolutely shocking!" squeaked Prissy.

"Disgusting," agreed Tilly Losh. "No wonder the mayor's so fat if he can afford to throw all that away."

"And we pay for it, you know," Prissy added.

"I don't," Tilly said.

"Yes, you do," Prissy snorted. "We have to pay to have a mayor, you know. We have to pay for his big grand house, and his gold chain, and even his toothpaste."

"I never knew that!" said Tilly.

"Well, you wouldn't, would you?" snooted Prissy. "You never even went to school. I had to do reading and sums and drawing. Anyway, we'd better go back to the café for our little gossip. We've got lots to talk about."

At a corner table, sat Boomer, their big gorilla friend. He was trying out bananas with mustard and bananas with tomato ketchup. When he saw the two dolls, he leapt over the table and hugged them hugely.

"My curls!" blushed Prissy. "I've just had them done."

"So sorry," said Boomer, giving her another, smaller hug.

"We came in here to talk about things," explained Prissy.

"Jolly good," munched Boomer.

"We noticed that Moggy is very prowly at the moment, and we just wondered why."

"Did you?" said Boomer. "Banana with mustard is super, on the other hand, banana with tomato ketchup is brilliant. BRILLIANT!"

"And then," Prissy battled on, "we saw all this waste in Mayor Bungle's bin – two whole chickens, half-a-dozen roast potatoes, a pawful of stuffing, half-a-dish of strawberry jelly and a slice of toast and marmalade."

"Really!" said Boomer. "Likes his food does the mayor. What I think really..."

"Yes?" said Prissy eagerly.

"What I think really is, bananas with mustard AND ketchup would be just delicious."

"Oh!" cried Prissy, exasperated.

Penguin, who had just waddled up, was more interested. He was cross-eyed so he saw twice as much as everybody else.

"Yes," he said, "I've seen Moggy prowling around more than usual. The first time I ever saw him, I thought he was just a black doormat. He didn't move for a whole week. I remember, I was just going to pick him up and put him in front of my fireplace when he sat up and scratched me."

"Savage!" said Prissy.

"Perhaps he's job hunting, or something like that," said Penguin, and waddled away.

"Cats don't go job hunting!" scoffed Prissy.

But nevertheless, she got out of bed quite early the following morning and went spying again on Moggy. To her astonishment, there he was, outside Mrs Bizzy's shop. He had his nose flattened against the shop window and his green eyes were staring. Just inside was a noticeboard with all sorts of little cards which said things like, "For Sale" or "Wanted". Suddenly, Moggy streaked off across the attic and seemed to be quite excited about something.

WANTED
WANTED

"Now what can THAT be about?" wondered Prissy. And she rushed over to the noticeboard to see for herself.

There was a budgie for sale; that was hardly exciting... And a three-wheeler bicycle. Somebody wanted a pair of slippers and a warm dressing gown. That would probably be Oxfam, the old bear who had just arrived in the attic and who had no warming fluff left on him at all. Then Prissy spotted the notice she was sure Moggy had been looking at. It said:

"Oh, my goodness!" shrieked Prissy. "I didn't know we had a witch in the attic!" And she tore round to Tilly Losh's house and knocked on the door in a frenzy.

"Get up!" she shouted. "I've got some terrible news."

"Perhaps we ought to tell the mayor," cried Tilly when she had been told, "I bet he didn't know either that we had a witch living up here."

"Just an old fairy story, I'll bet," grumbled Mayor Bungle, with his mouth full of egg and bacon. He hated to be disturbed when he was having his breakfast, coffee, lunch, afternoon tea, dinner or his bedtime drink. "If there was REALLY a witch round about, I'd have heard about it," he said.

But Prissy and Tilly Losh were not one bit sure about that. It was possible there MIGHT be a witch's house in the very far corner of the attic where a low beam came down.

Moggy had been prowling a long time, and still he had not found the witch's house. He sniffed the ground and measured small spaces with his whiskers. He wondered if he would have to pass an exam to be a witch's cat, and wondered too if the witch would feed him well. That was very important. He wondered what kind of work he would have to do. None, he hoped. Probably he could just sit on her doorstep looking mean and nasty.

He was tired, for he had been wandering all day. Also it seemed to be getting very dark, and that was because he was coming to the forest of glum trees. The glum forest looked oddly like a row of clothes rails, hung with coats and shawls and fluffy scarves which shook with papery upside-down bats, all bouncing up and down on their long pieces of elastic. The papery bats didn't look very friendly. And they weren't. They seemed to think it was funny to tweak Moggy's fur, and the more he miaowed, the more amused they were.

Moggy began to wish he hadn't strayed so far away from his own part of the attic. This faraway corner of it looked dismal and dark. And where an enormous dusty beam swept down to the floor, he could see a small boxy house of sorts. It had a sign saying, "Cobweb Cottage" hanging on the gate. The doorknocker was an old bone. To Moggy, it look horribly like a cat's bone.

He was about to run away when the door opened and an old woman peered out at him. She was so skinny she looked like a pile of bones held together with black rags. Her hair was like a dirty old hearthrug tied on to her head by a crooked hat.

"I've come to the wrong place!" gasped Moggy.

"I like a cat who tells terrible lies!" grinned the witch. "Come in." And she grabbed Moggy by his ears and hurled him into an armchair.

"Oh, golly!" thought Moggy. "What's she going to do with me now?"

"So you've come for the job, have you?" asked Witch Skinny Bones.

"I'm not sure," mumbled Moggy.

"Oh, I like a cat who's not sure," cackled Witch Skinny Bones.

"I probably have to pass an exam," sighed Moggy. "I'm not good at exams. I might just as well go home now."

"Oh, I LOVE cats who make up really

KEEP OUT
SPELLS
Cobweb Cot

silly excuses." The witch rolled round the floor like a demented skittle and laughed herself silly. It wasn't a nice sort of laugh.

"Lights out at ten," she snapped, suddenly, "and no midnight prowling about."

"Aren't I going to get any supper?" asked Moggy.

"I've had mine," said Witch Skinny Bones, disappearing upstairs to her bed.

Moggy tried to escape through the door, but there was a massive spider sitting on the doorknob and it said, "No one escapes Witch Skinny Bones unless she says so."

"Do you always do what the old witch tells you?" asked Moggy.

"Yes, I do," said the massive spider, rather astonished. NOT doing what he was told was something he had never even thought about.

Next day, Witch Skinny Bones got up early. It was about midday.

"Aren't I going to get any breakfast?" complained Moggy.

"I've had mine," said the witch. "The massive spider brought it up to me. I had corn-flakes and crunchy beetles. You're always talking about food. I adore a cat with a healthy appetite."

"Do you?" muttered Moggy, feeling horribly faint with hunger.

"Look," said Witch Skinny Bones, "if you're going to sulk every time you miss a meal, go and catch a bat from one of my glum trees. You can roast it, or fry it, or boil it in a pan, but don't expect ME to look after you. This is not a posh hotel."

Moggy thought of the home he had left and the cream cake in Prissy's bin, of the cucumber sandwich with one bite out of it in Tilly's and most of all, he thought about Mayor Bungle's bin where only the other day he had discovered two whole chickens, half-a-dozen roast potatoes, a pawful of stuffing, half-a-dish of strawberry jam and a slice of toast and marmalade – and he wished he had never thought of getting a job.

• CHAPTER TWO •

The Curly Spell

"NOW THEN," said Witch Skinny Bones, "I've been making plans. There's a big fat man in the Town Hall called Mayor Bungle, and I don't like him. When I was a young girl and very beautiful," the witch went on, "I entered a beauty competition and the mayor gave the prize to the Duchess of Snoot instead of to me."

Both of Moggy's whiskers twitched. The Duchess of Snoot was Prissy's aunt, and she had never been beautiful either. In fact, it would have been difficult to decide who had the ugliest face – the Duchess of Snoot or Witch Skinny Bones.

"Just because she was a stuck-up duchess," Skinny Bones went on, "AND she had a face like a squashed cabbage! So I want to get my own back on that stupid mayor. I reckon he must be blind, giving first prize to a squashed old cabbage."

Moggy was shocked and didn't know what to say.

"I love a cat who's shocked and doesn't know what to say," mocked the witch.

All this time, Moggy wondered why the witch wanted him and what it was going to be like being a witch's cat.

Skinny Bones soon told him.

"I'm going to make up a horrible spell and make Mayor Bungle sorry he ever gave that beauty prize to the Duchess of Snoot.

You must go out far and wide and find the things I need."

"Oh, good!" thought Moggy. "Once I get far and wide, I can run home."

"I'll send the massive spider with you," Witch Skinny Bones was saying, "because he knows the way. He knows every nook and cranny in this attic."

Moggy's heart sank at that. "Perhaps I could have a bite to eat before I go?" he said.

"I'm not hungry," the witch said. "Besides, cats should never eat between meals. It's bad for their whiskers. I daresay that's why you only have two left."

Moggy felt too dizzy to answer.

"The first thing I want you to fetch," continued Witch Skinny Bones, "is three squelch snakes. Bring them back in this bag – and choose fresh ones."

Poor Moggy trembled with fright. The wriggly, rubbery squelch snakes lived on the edge of Puddle Pond, and Oxfam and

Tilly Losh had had a frightful adventure with them and had been very lucky to get back alive.

"I like a cat who trembles with fright," giggled Witch Skinny Bones. "It keeps him on his paws and stops him falling asleep all day."

The massive spider opened the door and led Moggy through the glum trees and off towards Puddle Pond.

When the squelch snakes saw Moggy

coming, they thought he would make a horrible dinner – all tufty fluff and no fat on him, but he was better than nothing. The massive spider looked juicier. But the massive spider was not stupid. He spun a web over the pond and told Moggy to lower himself down and grab the first three snakes he could reach.

"Grab them by their tails," he said. "That end doesn't bite."

Terrified, Moggy hung from the web and snatched wildly at the squelchers. They ducked and dived, and slithered and squirmed, but at last he had three of them and crawled back across the web.

"Very good!" said the witch, when Moggy handed them over. "I only want the poison from their tongues, then the bad-tempered creatures can go home." The three snakes wriggled away – FURIOUS.

"Could I have some supper now?" gasped Moggy.

"Yes, you could have done if you'd come home in time. I don't cook for latecomers. What does it say on that notice?"

THIS KITCHEN CLOSES AT 6 o'clock

read Moggy, miserably.

He reckoned he wouldn't be a witch's cat for much longer because he'd be just a pile of fluff and bones. Oh, WHY had he thought his dear little home was boring?

Why had he thought Prissy was a silly doll, Tilly Losh was cheeky, Penguin was cross-eyed, Boomer was too bouncy and Oxfam was just a shabby, bumbling old bear? Even the mice, uncooked, seemed attractive.

He had just fallen asleep when Witch Skinny Bones screeched, "Wake up, you lazy brute! I need more messages."

"I suppose I've just missed breakfast," yawned Moggy.

"I admire a cat who

supposes correctly," spat Witch Skinny Bones. "I see you're getting used to my little ways."

She gave Moggy another shopping list.

"Climb up a glum tree and catch some bats," it said, "and be careful not to drop any of them on the way home." "If you drop a single one, my spell mixture will not work," the witch warned.

Climbing up a glum tree was not very easy. The trunk was very slippery. When the upside-down bats saw their home was being all scratched and their hiding place torn to rags by Moggy's claws, they were not at all pleased and pecked and scratched Moggy unmercifully.

"Be careful not to drop one," warned the massive spider, "or the spell mixture will not work."

"I wish I could drop the lot!" moaned Moggy. "I'm going bald!"

"You've done well again," Witch Skinny Bones greeted Moggy.

Moggy didn't bother to ask for any supper.

The witch shook the bats into her magic spell mixture and stirred them around until they were dizzy. Then she let them go.

"But now they've nowhere to live," cried Moggy. "I've wrecked their home."

"They'll find an empty glum tree somewhere," snapped the witch, "and if they don't, they'll just have to share, same as we do."

"Perhaps two's a crowd," muttered Moggy, hopefully. "I think it's time I went home."

"I'm fond of a cat who can tell the time," sniggered Witch Skinny Bones.

"Just one more thing to finish the mixture," she said. "I need one of Prissy's curls."

"Oh, no!" wailed Moggy, "I couldn't do THAT!"

"Couldn't, or won't?" growled the witch, looking fearsome. "Why did you apply to be a witch's cat if you don't want to do nasty things?"

"I thought I would just have to sit on your doormat looking mean and spiteful."

"Huh! I worship a cat who makes whopping big mistakes!" tittered Witch Skinny Bones.

The unhappy cat set off across the attic and the massive spider went with him. Moggy started to run, because he thought if he could get rid of the spider, he would be able to sneak home and not have to get one of Prissy's curls. But the massive spider had eight legs and could run fast very easily.

"You shouldn't have

tried that," it said. "The witch would be very cross if I let you escape."

When they arrived at Prissy's house, she was sitting in her garden sunbathing. Next to her sat the mayor, telling her how utterly delicious she looked.

"I like to take care of myself," blushed Prissy, patting her shining curls and swishing on some fresh lipstick. "I do think a lady should try to look nice at all times."

"Oh, yes, indeed!" agreed the mayor, swigging lots of lemonade and eating chocolate éclairs two at a time.

"I like to keep slim too," added Prissy, glancing at the mayor's enormous tummy.

"Oh, yes, indeed," said the mayor again, gobbling two more éclairs.

Moggy decided he must wait until dark before he would dare to snatch one of Prissy's curls. The witch had given him a pair of scissors with which to do the terrible deed. Perhaps he could go to the hairdresser's and find a spare curl on the floor. But the massive spider no doubt would tell tales.

"Oh dear!" yawned Prissy, patting her little mouth, "I do believe I must say good evening to you, Mayor Bungle."

"Indeed, indeed!" gushed the mayor, "You must get your beauty sleep." And he waddled off.

Prissy tidied up the dishes, plumped the cushion which the mayor had squashed, and went to bed.

That night, the moon did not come out. It was tired and fell asleep behind a cloud.

"Good!" thought Moggy. "It will be easier to steal a curl if the moon is not looking."

The massive spider climbed up the drainpipe to Prissy's window and left one of his silky cobweb ropes for Moggy.

When they peeped through the bedroom window, they were astonished at what they saw, Prissy was fast asleep and she was absolutely BALD. On the bedpost hung a wig of golden curls.

"My goodness me!" gasped Moggy. "If the other toys knew about this! The beautiful Prissy, old and bald!"

The bad cat prowled across the bedroom floor on his tummy and snipped a large curl from the middle of the wig and slid off into the night, feeling quite ashamed of himself.

"Excellent!" cried the witch when she saw the curl. "If I'd known you were going to be back so fast, I'd have saved you some breakfast." She tossed the curl into the spell mixture and whizzed it round furiously, shrieking,

"Squelch a bat,
This and that,
Mix it with a curl.
Stir it with a wooden spoon,
And give it one more whirl."

When it was done, the mixture looked like chocolate, and it smelt delicious.

Moggy felt faint with hunger. He had not eaten for days.

"Not for you, my black pussy cat," cackled Witch Skinny Bones. "This is for Mayor Bungle." And she rolled the mixture into pretty little shapes and placed them in a golden box tied with red ribbon.

"It's the mayor's birthday tomorrow," she chortled, rolling round the kitchen like a sausage roll gone mad. "Post them through his letter box," she told Moggy, "and don't bother to come back. I hate a cat who expects feeding all the time."

Joyfully, Moggy ran off through the glum trees, and all the way home. The massive spider did not follow him.

His dear little house was just as he'd left it: messy, and very homely. The cupboard was still full of food, and his bed was warm and fluffy.

• CHAPTER THREE •

The Horrible Birthday Present

PRISSY AWOKE with a loud shriek. It was so loud that Tilly Losh came running.

"My dear!" she gasped. "Whatever is the matter?"

"Nothing!" screamed Prissy. "Please go away. I was having a nightmare, that's all."

When Tilly had gone, Prissy stared at

herself in the mirror, panic-stricken. The curl on the top of her head, her very best curl, was missing.

"I know!" she thought. "I have been attacked by an eagle in the middle of the night. I KNEW it was not safe to sleep with the window open. I might have known that one night I would be attacked by a crazy eagle. It had to happen one day. Oh my!"

Tilly Losh ran round the attic telling everyone that Prissy had had a terrible nightmare.

"The poor lady," said the mayor, who was munching cornflakes and didn't really want to know.

"Perhaps she has had too many late parties," said Boomer. "I'll go and give her a big hug."

Prissy was not in the mood for a big hug, and with one eye through the letter box, she begged Boomer to call another time.

"It's just a tiny headache," she squeaked.

Penguin brought a few ice cubes from his bathtub, but Prissy wailed that ice cubes could not possibly help. NOTHING could help.

Witch Skinny Bones, who was peeping down the chimney, laughed so much, she nearly rolled off the roof.

"How am I ever going to go out again?" sobbed Prissy. "How am I going to give my little dinner parties or dance with the mayor?"

The only thing to do was find something that would hide the bald patch. She dived into her wardrobe and rummaged feverishly. Out came a glittering silver dress – her Christmas Day dress, half-a-dozen lacy blouses, heavily encrusted with embroidery, silk stockings, a dear little fan, and last of all, a very large pink hat. Gratefully, Prissy put it on.

Unfortunately, the hat had once belonged to her aunt, the Duchess of Snoot. It was several sizes too large and made Prissy look like a walking umbrella on two small legs. But at least she was now able to go down to Mrs Bizzy's shop for her groceries.

"Good morning,"

said Mrs Bizzy to the walking umbrella.

"A bag of jelly babies, please," said Prissy.

"Oh, it's YOU!" exclaimed Mrs Bizzy. "I didn't recognise you."

Prissy paid for the jelly babies and walked out in a huff.

Tilly Losh stared curiously at the umbrella as it tottered past.

"Nice day," greeted Prissy.

"Oh," said Tilly Losh. "I didn't see you under that enormous hat. Why are you wearing it?"

"My goodness me!" scoffed Prissy. "It's the very latest fashion. Didn't you know that?"

"No, I didn't know that," admitted Tilly Losh.

"Well, of course, you wouldn't, would you?" snooted Prissy. "I keep forgetting you never went to school. ALL the young ladies in my school wore hats like this."

"Really?" cried Tilly. "I'm surprised they

could see where they were going. I'm amazed they would see to do their sums, and reading and drawing."

Prissy was beginning to get very cross, but she smiled sweetly, and said, "We were TAUGHT how to wear big hats, and do sums, reading and drawing at the same time. It was good manners to wear a hat."

"Fancy!" said Tilly Losh. "I see."

Which was more than poor Prissy could do.

Moggy was shocked. What terrible thing had he done? Then he remembered the mayor's birthday present and quickly posted it through the Town Hall letter box.

"Oh, whoopee! Choccies!" cried the mayor when he saw the large golden box, tied with a red ribbon. "These must be from someone who loves me; Prissy, perhaps." And he gobbled them up greedily.

"I seem to be losing weight!" he exclaimed, as his tummy began to shrink. "Isn't that good! I can scoff chocolates and still get thinner. But I seem to be getting smaller too," he said. "NOT so jolly good. Oh, NO!" he screamed. "I'm disappearing altogether!"

The gold chain he was wearing fell off his neck and clunked in a heap onto the floor.

In a panic, the mayor scuttled to his mirror and was just big enough to see that he had turned into a horrid black beetle.

"I expect I'm just having a bad dream," he laughed. "I'll wake up in a minute and it will be lunchtime."

But a long nose appeared

over the windowsill, and then two beady eyes, and a voice cackled:

"Happy birthday, Mayor Bungle. Did you enjoy my yummy magic chocolates?"

"Oh, cripes!" screeched the mayor. "It's Witch Skinny Bones! I remember now – I gave you first prize at the beauty competition many years ago. You were so beautiful!" he lied.

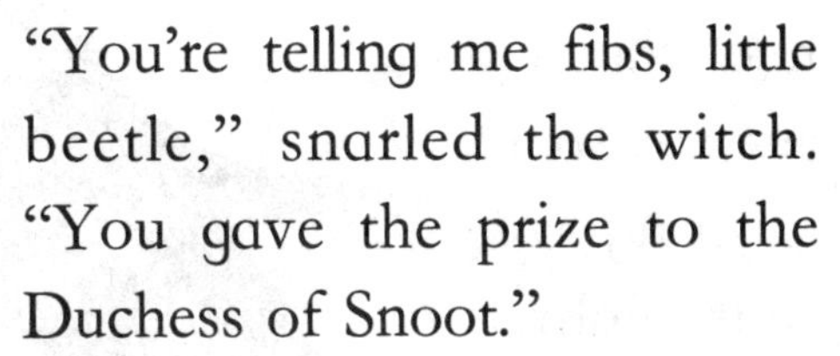

"You're telling me fibs, little beetle," snarled the witch. "You gave the prize to the Duchess of Snoot."

"What! That ugly lady with the face like a squashed cabbage? Never!" The mayor turned pale and rattled with fear inside his little black shell.

But Witch Skinny Bones just hooted and flew off, and her laughter could be heard as far away as the glum trees. It rattled the branches and brought roof tiles tumbling.

Miserably, Mayor Bungle tried to put on his gold chain again, but it just kept falling off. Then he remembered with horror that he had called an important meeting for that night. Calling meetings was what he loved doing best. This one was about keeping the attic tidy: Moggy was always dropping fish bones on the floor, Penguin tossed away biscuit papers, Boomer left banana skins on the pavement and Tilly Losh threw everything everywhere. Only Prissy remembered to put her rubbish in the bin. But then one would expect that from a lady who had been to school, and been taught how to wear a big hat.

Tilly and Prissy were in the café again, trying out the toasted crumpets and wondering what to gossip about. Prissy was feeling around the table for the butter.

"Is it good manners to wear a big hat even indoors?" asked Tilly Losh.

"Oh, certainly," said Prissy. "Especially if one is taking afternoon tea."

"Oh," said Tilly. But she wondered why she had seen Prissy having breakfast in it, and doing her dusting in it and hanging out her clothes in it. She also noticed that whenever she even mentioned the hat, Prissy would fly into a terrible tantrum and march off.

"By the way," said Tilly, "Moggy's back. I wonder where he's been? He looks terribly skinny. He's probably overdone the prowling."

"That's odd," said Prissy. "I'm sure I saw him peeping at me when I was doing my dusting. And then I fancied I saw him hiding in my hedge while I was hanging out the washing."

"He's probably interested in your hat," decided Tilly.

In the evening, everyone wandered across the attic to the Town Hall. Nobody wanted to go, because the meeting was about being tidy and they knew that the mayor would ENJOY ticking them off.

"A gorilla MY age shouldn't HAVE to get ticked off," Boomer grumbled.

"And I can't help dribbling sawdust on the ground," Oxfam sighed. "I'm sure the mayor wouldn't like moth holes in HIS head."

But the mayor was having problems of his own.

He had arrived at the Town Hall early and had spent the last two hours struggling to climb up the leg of his chair.

"I wonder why the mayor's so late?" asked Tilly Losh.

"Good evening, everybody," squeaked the mayor.

"Who said that?" asked Boomer.

"I didn't," said Penguin.

The mice all shook their heads.

"We've come here tonight to talk about tidiness," the mayor struggled on. The toys looked around everywhere, but they couldn't see anyone.

"Someone's playing stupid tricks," snapped Prissy. "This is no joking matter."

"I think it's funny," giggled Tilly Losh.

Then the mice all began to titter.

The mayor started to shake with rage. "Silence!" he bellowed in a tiny wee voice.

"Oh, look!" cried Boomer, "there's a horrid black beetle sitting on the mayor's chair. THAT's why he won't sit on it." And he swept it off with his big hairy paw.

Mayor Bungle felt himself flying through space. It seemed as if he was flying for ever. The furniture all looked upside down; the floor looked like the ceiling and the toys were like giants. As soon as he landed, he scuttled into a hole in the skirting board and lay there, trembling.

"Happy birthday, dear Bungle,

happy birthday to you!" chuckled Witch Skinny Bones.

"Well!" said Boomer. "Fancy old Bungle forgetting to come!"

"Awfully odd," agreed Prissy. But she was glad, because she was feeling sillier and sillier in her hat.

Only Moggy knew what dreadful thing had happened to the poor mayor, and it was all HIS fault that Prissy had to walk around looking like an umbrella, and that the mayor had been turned into an unimportant small creature. He did not want to be a bad cat any more.

Next day, he went back through the glum trees and knocked on the witch's door. Witch Skinny Bones was knitting a tea cosy out of pink worms. The worms didn't like being knitted and they kept squirming off the needles. They didn't want to have to sit on a hot teapot either. When the witch got up to answer the door, they wriggled away into the garden.

"And what do YOU want?" she spat.

"I'm sorry I've been a bad cat," said Moggy. "I want you to give Prissy her curl back and take the spell off Mayor Bungle, please."

"Please as much as you like!" snorted Witch Skinny Bones, and slammed the door.

Moggy slunk home, and he wiped his eyes with his paws. He was still blowing his nose, when in walked the massive spider.

"I've run away from home," he said. "I'm tired of that old bag of bones. She's too mean."

He was carrying Prissy's curl and a scrap of paper torn from the witch's spell book.

"I've got the 'undoing spell'," he told Moggy.

The undoing spell was very easy. All they needed were tea leaves and sugar scrambled together.

The spell said:

Mix and munch,
Stir and crunch,
Sprinkle with dust,
Cough if you must,
But never NEVER sneeze.

"That's very silly," laughed Moggy, but he said the magic words.

Then he and the massive spider went to the Town Hall and scattered the magic mixture outside the hole in the skirting board.

"Oh, joy!" trembled the mayor, "there's a

smell out there of eggs and bacon and sausage and mushroom and fried bread!" And he scurried out and gobbled up the wonderful mixture. At once, he blew up to his normal size.

"It must have been a nightmare after all," he told himself. But he wasn't quite sure.

When it was dark, Moggy and the massive spider climbed back into Prissy's bedroom and glued back the curl.

"Oh, heaven!" cried Prissy when she got up next morning and saw that the wig was mended. "It must have grown again during the night!"

She dashed out to Mrs Bizzy's shop, for there were lots of things she needed.

Tilly Losh was buying a duster, which was extremely unusual.

"Where's your hat?" she asked.

"Oh, hats went out of fashion yesterday. Didn't you know that?" scorned Prissy.

"No, I didn't know that," Tilly Losh answered. And she stared closely at Prissy's curl where a tiny patch of glue was shining in the sunlight, but she didn't mention it.

And neither did anyone else.

• CHAPTER FOUR •

Getting Rid of Witch Skinny Bones

WHEN WITCH Skinny Bones discovered that the massive spider had escaped, and worse, stolen back Prissy's curl and the "undoing spell", she was absolutely FURIOUS. She came squealing into the attic, stamping and shouting and frightening all the toys. Everybody went inside and locked their doors. Mrs Bizzy closed her shop, and the mayor hung up a notice saying:

NO MEETING TONIGHT

When the witch had gone away, everyone came out again and talked about what they should do.

"We could call in the army," said Moggy.

The head of the army was the Grand Old Duke of York. He had ten thousand men. Every day, he marched them up to the top of the hill, and then he marched them down again. Everyone thought this was very silly, because there was absolutely NOTHING at the top of the hill. If

there had been a café, the soldiers could have stopped for a cup of tea and a sandwich, perhaps. But there wasn't, so they couldn't. They grumbled and puffed and complained like mad. But the Grand Old Duke of York just bellowed,

"It's GOOD for you, you 'orrible lot!"

The soldiers couldn't see why it was good for them; they wanted to go to war and shoot their

cannons at the enemy. They had great piles of used matchsticks which they could fire as far away as the other side of the attic.

But all they ever did was polish their boots and march to the top of the hill, and then all the way down again.

Then along came a little crowd of toys with Boomer at the front. "Oh, goody!" thought the soldiers. "There must be some bother."

Boomer told the Grand Old Duke of York about Witch Skinny Bones and what a nuisance she was being. Some of the soldiers turned pale. They had never dared to march as far as the glum trees. Perhaps marching up and down the hill was rather jolly after all. Maybe, if they promised not to be so rough, Mayor Bungle would build them a café on the top of the hill and then they would LOVE marching up it. The Grand Old Duke wasn't very delighted to hear the news either. He had rather hoped that the toys had come about an outbreak of chickenpox, or an escaped cow, or something like that.

"Have no fear, dear chap," he said to

Boomer. "We will see to it tomorrow. It's rather too dark now."

Next day, the Grand Old Duke of York said, "Oh, dearie me, it looks like rain. I don't want my soldiers slithering around in the mud. They'll get their boots filthy."

The day after that, he declared that he could feel snow in the air, "If the slightest bit of ice got into the cannons, they just wouldn't fire, and THEN what!?"

"Perhaps you'll all get sunburnt tomorrow," scoffed Moggy.

"Don't mention sunburn!" gasped the Grand Old Duke. "When we were down by the Indian Ocean last week, the sun was so hot we came back like fried sausages."

Witch Skinny Bones, who listened in to everyone all the time, thought it was all very funny. No one would dare to come near her house. She sat up in bed with her spell book and giggled as she read all the wonderful naughty things she could do if she wanted to. She could change the toys into anything she liked. And she DID like.

"Gosh! What fun I could have," cackled the old witch. She could change the toys into piles of rags, hard-boiled eggs, spotted toadstools or squashed bananas. And the soldiers could all be turned into tin. That would be a great joke. She could make the Grand Old Duke of York into a statue and stand him in the middle of the attic, and everyone who walked past would say, "Ha ha! HE wasn't much good. He was scared stiff of a poor old woman."

Then Prissy put on one of her prettiest dresses and set off to see the Duke.

"You're so awfully brave," she told him. "Only YOU would dare to go near that dreadful old witch. I should be terrified."

The Duke twiddled his moustache and puffed out his chest.

"My dear lady," he said, "you were born to be a delicate and gracious lady. I was

born to be a fierce and daring soldier."

"Oh, yes, indeed!" agreed Prissy, trying hard to make her eyelashes flutter. "And I expect you have made lots of exciting plans on how you are going to capture that horrid old witch."

"Oh, magnificent plans!" blustered the Grand Old Duke, trying hard to think what they were.

With the thought of the beautiful Prissy still in his head, the Old Duke leapt straight into his boots at the very crack of dawn and woke up his soldiers.

"Oh, sir," they grumbled, "it's a bit early

to be marching up to the top of the hill, isn't it?"

"We're not marching up the hill today," bellowed the Duke. "We're marching to the glum trees."

"I've got a tummy ache," moaned one of the soldiers.

"No tummy aches allowed!" roared the Grand Old Duke of York. "Get your boots on and bring the cannons."

The cannons hadn't been used for a long time, and they squeaked and rattled across the attic floor. The upside-down bats heard them coming a mile off and swooped down on the soldiers furiously.

"Oh, Mummy!" cried the soldier who had a tummy ache.

"Fire the cannons!" commanded the Duke. "Pepper the brutes with matchsticks!"

To his great surprise, the bats didn't like that at all and they all flew away.

"Golly!" thought the Duke. "Going to be easier than I thought. I should have done it years ago. What a wonderful thing it is to be a brave and glorious soldier. I expect I'll get a big medal for this – or maybe half-a-dozen. Yes, half-a-dozen would be nice: all different colours."

The gorgeous Prissy would be bound to fall in love with him then, if indeed she hadn't already.

"Fire a bit more!" he yelled.

Witch Skinny Bones was munching cornflakes and thinking: "That silly Old Duke of York and his ten thousand men will be here in a minute." She spread some marmalade on a piece of toast and cackled.

"I suppose he thinks he's going to frighten me! I expect he thinks he's going to tell his soldiers to go 'Bang Bang' with their worn-out old matchsticks and I'm going to flop down dead. Oops a flippin' daisy!" She wiped her mouth on the tablecloth and thumbed through her spell book.

Meanwhile, the soldiers were marching nearer and nearer. Their boots were going clomp, clomp, clomp.

The Grand Old Duke knocked boldly on the witch's door.

"Oh, good morning, Your Yorkship," greeted Witch Skinny Bones. "You and your men must be very tired after all that marching and shooting."

"We are rather," panted the Duke, a bit surprised. He could smell toast and marmalade.

"Have some," wheedled Witch Skinny Bones.

The smell was so delicious, the Duke and his soldiers forgot for the moment what they'd come for, and sat down.

"On your way to war, are you?" asked the witch slyly, spreading the marmalade thickly.

"Mmmm, straight after breakfast," mumbled the Duke. He should have known that the witch was not really being kind. She had, of course, cast a spell on the marmalade.

"All this marching has made my bones feel stiff," said the soldier with the tummy ache.

"Mine too," said the others.

"Ouch!" was the last thing the Grand Old Duke of York cried as his arms and legs stopped working.

He and the whole army had turned into tin soldiers. Some had their rifles over their shoulders. Some were kneeling and pointing their guns. And some of them were lying on their tummies, trying to take aim. The

Duke himself was saluting, and staring at nothing.

"How smart my garden looks now," tittered the witch. "Better than boring old garden gnomes!"

The massive spider was spying from the chimney pot, and he skittled across the attic to tell the toys what had happened.

"That silly old Duke!" scoffed Tilly Losh.

Because Penguin was cross-eyed, he could see things from both sides.

"I suppose he did his best," he said. "Perhaps WE could think of a plan."

"Oh, yes!" said Prissy. "Like WHAT, for instance? Should we go and attack her with a feather duster?"

"We'll have to trick her," said Boomer.

Moggy, who felt it was all his fault, said that the very best thing to do would be to steal Witch Skinny Bones's spell book, then they could think up some super plans. He agreed to go with the massive spider and wait until the witch was in bed.

The tins soldiers stood, or knelt, or lay, glinting in the moonlight. They were all wide awake, but they could not move. The

witch, however, seemed to be fast asleep. She was snoring so loudly, the chimney pot was wobbling. Her grey woolly hair flew around on the pillow in the draught that was coming from her mouth, and her old yellow teeth rattled in the glass of water at her bedside. She looked horrid.

Unfortunately, Witch Skinny Bones slept with the spell book under her pillow. Every time Moggy tried to tweak it out with his paws, the witch's mouth fluttered and she opened one eye.

"That's only her glass eye," whispered the massive spider. "She's not really looking at you."

"She LOOKS as if she's looking," shivered Moggy.

Then Witch Skinny Bones shuddered and turned over like a giant skinny whale, and Moggy was able to grab the spell book easily.

Everyone went to Boomer's house, and

they read the spell book from beginning to end with lots of gasps of horror – and some giggles.

Tilly Losh liked the spell about the roly-poly pudding. It gave her an idea. They would roll Witch Skinny Bones into a parcel and post her down to Somewhere. Then, she would never come back.

"I've got an old carpet," said Prissy. "It's real Persian, but I was going to give it to the bin man."

The toys had seen Prissy buying the carpet from Mrs Bizzy's shop for ten pence, but they said nothing.

"We'll somehow have to get the witch to lie down on them," said Penguin.

"IT," corrected Prissy, "We've only got one carpet."

"Oh, really?" blushed Penguin, squinting more than ever.

Boomer had to scratch his head to help him to think. "Perhaps if we all pretend to be sunbathing on little mats, and leave the big one empty, the witch might come and like that one," he suggested.

"Why?" asked Penguin.

"Because she's greedy," explained Boomer.

So the dolls all put on their swimsuits and lay down. All except Prissy, who first had to find her frilly pink suit and a pair of sunglasses before coming out looking radiant.

Sure enough, Witch Skinny Bones came

stomping across the attic in a terrible rage. She wanted to find out who had stolen her spell book. Without it, she was quite helpless.

The toys heard her coming and they trembled, but they pretended not to notice and lay with their eyes shut tight.

"What are all YOU lot doing there?" screeched Witch Skinny Bones, surprised that they weren't running away in a fright.

"Just sunbathing," said Prissy sleepily, and not opening her eyes.

"I want to do that!" the witch sulked. "I want to sunbathe too."

"Sorry. There's no room," Prissy said.

"There is," the witch stamped. "There's that big carpet in the middle."

"Oh, you can't lie on THAT one!" gasped Prissy. "It's real Persian!"

"I'll lie on it then," snapped the witch.

And she did.

At once, the dolls swooped on her and rolled her up like a roly-poly pudding. Witch Skinny Bones struggled frantically and shrieked and scratched.

"Push her noses back in!" cried cross-eyed Penguin.

Prissy fetched brown paper, and Boomer had some string he used when mountaineering down the Mountain Stairs.

When they were finished, the toys took the terrible parcel to Mrs Bizzy, who weighed it and put on the stamps. She also glued on a little label which said:

DO NOT HANDLE WITH CARE

Puff Puff drove the parcel to the station at the top of the Mountain Stairs and let it roll down to Somewhere.

"Hah!" said Prissy. "It feels like time for tea now."

"What about the Grand Old Duke of York and his ten thousand men?" asked Moggy. "We've got all the 'undoing spells'."

"We'll undo them tomorrow," yawned Prissy.

"Yes, soon enough," agreed all the toys.

Moggy curled up with his fish bones. He had been a bad cat, but at least he had helped to get rid of the horrid witch. He fell asleep and had his favourite dream – the one about mice, tossed in butter and served with mushrooms.